A THOUSAND FIENDISH ANGELS

A Thousand Fiendish Angels.
Copyright © J.F. Penn (2013, 2019). All rights reserved.

www.JFPenn.com

ISBN: 978-1-912105-98-4

Requests to publish work from this book should be sent to:
joanna@CurlUpPress.com

Cover and Interior Design: JD Smith Design

Printed by Lightning Source

www.CurlUpPress.com

A THOUSAND FIENDISH ANGELS

STORIES INSPIRED BY DANTE'S INFERNO

J.F. PENN

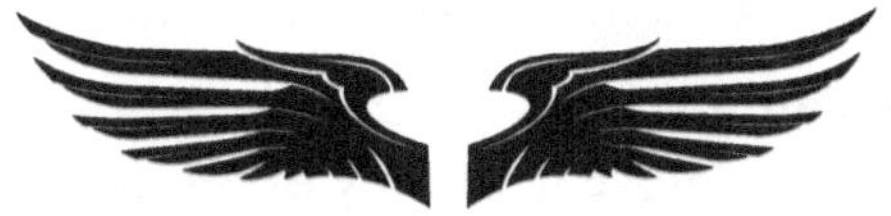

INTRODUCTION

"I saw more than a thousand fiendish angels
perching above the gates, enraged and screaming:
'Who is this one who comes, and without death,
dares walk into the kingdom of the dead?'"

Inferno Canto VIII, Dante Alighieri

THIS BOOK CONTAINS THREE short stories inspired by Dante's *Inferno*, linked by a book of human skin passed down through generations.

Sins of the Flesh

When the mutilated corpse of a wealthy author is discovered, the police officer sent to investigate finds a curious diary amongst the occult objects at the scene.

Will he uncover the author's secret at the ruined chapel, and can he pay the price that it demands?

Sins of Treachery

On the death of their Grandfather, twin brothers Simon and Gestas are left a map covered in alchemical symbols that could lead them to great wealth and power.

But they find more than they expected in the frozen wastes of the Arctic north …

Sins of Violence

In a brutal post-apocalyptic world, a young girl is about to be taken to The Minotaur for a Blessing that will end her innocence.

Can her sister gain access to the fortified city of Dis in time to stop the ritual and avenge her own lost youth?

CHAPTER 1:
SINS OF THE FLESH

I LEFT THE HYSTERICAL housekeeper downstairs with my partner and strode up the wide staircase to the first floor, my feet sinking into the plush carpet, my hand clasping the burnished bronze railing to speed my journey on.

The call had come in towards the end of our shift, and I was keen to assess the scene quickly so I could get out of uniform and into the bar as fast as possible. Since Jeannie had left, I could no longer bear our meager apartment, a constant reminder of the myriad failings of my career and tainted love.

I reached the top of the stairs and paused to catch my breath, looking around at the oil paintings in gold frames, ornate vases and Persian rugs. I felt a pang of jealousy at the opulent riches of this man's kingdom. His smallest closet contained more than everything I own, but even rich men cannot escape what must come to us all, and affluence means nothing to a corpse.

The stink of death reached me as I turned towards a partially open door made of dark oak, intricately carved with symbols of alchemy and superstition. I bent to look closer and found every sign of protection engraved upon it: an inverted horseshoe, an Islamic charm to ward off the evil eye, and a Catholic saint holding up a cross in his right hand to guard against Satan's encroachment. A Jewish mezuzah of teal Venetian glass was nailed to the doorframe, its Holy verses on parchment scroll denying destructive agents access. This man had clearly tried everything to stop supernatural forces from reaching him, but the stench told me that death had crept in here regardless.

I was no stranger to the dead, but now I felt the need for that extra ounce of courage, for a curious dread had taken hold of me, a leaden coldness that spread through my limbs. I thought with longing of the hip flask hidden in the car outside, craving the swig of vodka to help focus my mind on the task ahead. I didn't want to see what was beyond the door, but I crushed down the insidious fear and reached to push it fully open.

The door creaked, and wind chimes jangled to scare away malicious spirits, the sound bringing an incongruous sense of life to the inert atmosphere.

I put my hand to my nose, trying unsuccessfully to mask the foul odor of voided bowels and rotting flesh. My sweeping gaze took in the lavish glamor of the room, then the dead body splayed wide on the antique four-poster bed. A naked man on white satin sheets, now hideously stained with bodily fluids, bulging flesh on a morbidly obese body lying in a vile slush of his own foul emissions. Christopher Faerwald had been a famous author who made millions from his novels, many of them adapted for the big screen, but he hadn't been seen in years. Now I understood why. His physical disfigurement had turned him into a recluse.

Accustomed to the stink now, I moved closer to the bed to examine the corpse. Flies rose into the air at my approach, swollen from feeding, indignant buzzing at my interruption of their feast. Tattooed words covered every inch of the man's bloated body. They may have been legible once when his skin was young and taut, but they had since morphed into grotesque shapes. Open vowels that threatened to swallow and sharp consonants, each angle cut deep into his flesh, all inked with a dark crimson stain.

Were the words written in his own blood? I shuddered at the thought, surely a fantastical idea awoken by this macabre den. The walls were covered in crucifixes and painted with pentacles, and ancient holy books cluttered the floor in overflowing piles as if he had tried to barricade himself in here.

The man's face was a rictus of horror, a gaping grimace, as if he had witnessed the denizens of Hell streaming out of the maw of Hades and died of terror to look upon them.

A thin scalpel and a mirror lay next to him on the bed, fallen from his hands as he carved more words into his forehead even as he died. It looked like the beginnings of a prayer for deliverance.

As I examined him more closely, I could see that strips of skin had been torn from his limbs leaving weeping open wounds, crawling with maggots that devoured his souring flesh. It looked like torture, yet there were no signs of forced entry and, according to the housekeeper, nothing had been taken from the man's store of great wealth. I turned to survey the opulent space.

The dying sun flooded through a pair of large bay windows, suffusing the room with a ruby glow and a touch of flame. Outside, thick purple clouds gathered in the dusk like blood blisters across the sky, the beginnings of an unseasonal storm evident in the rain that pattered against the window.

A wide mahogany desk looked out towards a small church that squatted on the edge of a wood. Faerwald's personal chapel, part of his vast estate out here on the edge of civilization. He had purchased this place before he rose to the heights of fame, buying luxury properties around the world with his riches. I'd rather be on the beaches of Monaco than holed up here to die in obscurity, but he had returned to his roots in the last years.

The wall to the right of his desk was devoted to erotic images, gorgeous art morphing into pornography. I couldn't help but look closer. Sandstone carvings from the Hindu temple of Khajuraho depicted orgies of debauchery, bodies entwined in yogic poses as they thrust and writhed together. A set of art-house black and white photographs revealed scenes from a dungeon, soft tongues soothing scarred and whipped bodies.

A small print caught my eye amongst the frenzied sensory overload. Naked human figures swept into a hellish vortex, embracing each other with desire even as they were sucked into oblivion. Circle of the Lustful by William Blake, I read in the text below. I couldn't help but glance back at the obscene figure spread-eagled on the bed, pushing away the repugnant image of this bloated body engaged in carnal acts. He was a shade of the handsome youth he had once been, a magnet for beautiful women, envied by men for his success. But beneath the mound of flesh, fattened from years of gluttony and excess, Faerwald's bones were still aristocratic.

I picked up a Hollywood-style photo frame from the desk. The picture within showed the author in a slim-fit white tuxedo, strong arms wrapped around a stunning young woman who smiled up at him with cornflower-blue eyes darkened with a hint of wanton pleasure. Envy surged within me, and the need to drink almost drove me back to the car, desperate to tip even the tiniest dribble into my mouth.

I pushed down the craving and turned to examine the desk, using my pen to flick open a leather diary in the center. On the final page, Faerwald's last words stared up at me, written in blood, diseased with tinges of purple and rusty clots that stained the thick ivory paper.

> *She comes tonight to claim what I promised in exchange so long ago.*
>
> *I didn't believe her words back then, didn't think at all. What she offered has come to pass, and yet still I struggle to believe that my soul can be taken from me. I know I must pay the price for my sin, but if I can, I will prevent another from falling as far as I have done.*
>
> *I have hidden the book so she must sleep again. It is buried, and I am finished, but perhaps this last act will earn me a sliver of redemption.*

His handwriting was measured, sane and deliberate, but the words read like one of his novels. Was Faerwald living within the realms of fantasy when he passed so violently into the next world? Yet as I looked over again at the man's horrified face, I knew that his agony had not been mere imagination.

Rain pattered on the window, and I looked out again to the chapel. Faerwald had sat here looking at it when he wrote those last words, and I felt a prickle of sensation, as if those murky portals called to me. Could he have buried the strange book inside?

Something dark began to uncoil within me. I would exchange much to experience the riches this man enjoyed in his lifetime.

I made my decision.

I ran back down the stairs, calling out to my partner that I needed to investigate further evidence outside. He shouted after me, but I ignored him, caught up in the sensation that I must get to the chapel, that time was of the essence.

As I stepped outside, the light rain morphed into icy sleet, and heavy purple clouds above me split open with forked lightning. Thunder rolled across the desolate space between the house and the chapel. I pulled my coat tighter, fighting against Nature, buffeted violently as opposing winds clashed all around. It was as if I pushed a great weight ahead of me into a squall sent from Hell itself to tear this somber valley apart.

Each step across the open ground was a huge effort, but when I finally made it to the lych-gate at the entrance to the tiny churchyard, the storm eased a little, the rain lighter, although the wind still howled around me.

The chapel was old and partly ruined. Stone blocks covered in lichen lay in the grass below gargoyles hanging skewed from the edges of broken masonry, their faces eaten away by time. The present facade seemed to be built upon a more archaic structure, stones that had perhaps been worshipped as pagan gods in the days before Christ.

The plants in the churchyard were withered, all color leached from them. They covered the earth in thick patches, rising up from around the edges of tombstones, nourished by the dead beneath. I had imagined that I was running to sanctuary, but now the oppressive and malevolent miasma of the place sank into my bones. I hesitated, yet I still wanted to enter, my curiosity deeply roused to search for the mysterious book.

The fury of the storm surged again, crackling with energy, wind whipping round in tornado spirals, lifting the heads of strange albino flowers to the sky. Dust and ashes blew into my eyes, painting the scene with the desolate grey of mourning. I rubbed them frantically to clear my vision and hurried into the porch, my face brushing against something soft as I stumbled out of the wet gloom. I reeled back to see a dead crow hung by the neck above me, blue-black feathers still adhering to decaying flesh, its eyes open and unseeing.

The great door opened with a sigh, the wind sucked inside, filling the void with the desolation of chill air.

I stepped through, my footfall stirring dust from the floor, the sound echoing around the deserted building. The light inside was an amethyst haze from the heavy storm clouds, barely penetrating the nave through intricate stained glass windows with images of tortured saints, martyred for the glory of their God. The chapel venerated death, rather than eternal life, and ahead of me, as if in homage, a life-size crucifix hung behind the altar. Christ's face was a skeletal version of the dead Faerwald, as if the Son of God could see what Hell awaited him beyond the veil.

My eyes dropped to the altar, draped in cloth that had once been pure white but which now hung in dirty, dismal tatters. As the holiest place in the building, it was surely the most fitting location to bury such a book. I walked towards it, across flagstones carved with the names of the dead. The words ran into each other like the broken letters on Faerwald's body, a mass grave of victims who perished together in some ancient plague.

I usually felt a calm peace within churches, a sense of something holy, but this place was malignant and hungry, taking each breath faster than I could exhale.

A pair of candlesticks coated in melted wax rested on the altar, the gold of their surface dulled by dust. I could just make out the twisted figures of crucified angels, their mouths open as they pleaded with a God who had deserted them.

In the centre of the altar was a box, a tabernacle for the Host, the bread of the Eucharist turned into Christ's body for the consumption of the faithful. I pushed the lid open to see a mass of crawling maggots within, their swollen white bodies wriggling over each other to get at the crumbs of wafer, an unholy miracle of rotting sustenance in this unnatural place.

Sensing that the book must be close, I knelt at the altar, and a momentary chink appeared in the madness that possessed me. My resolve wavered. I should walk away now, leave this chapel and be done with the place.

But other thoughts intruded – my sordid apartment, the neighbors who disturbed my sleep with their fighting, the debts I owed at the bar and my ever-growing need for vodka to keep the nightmares away. Below it all, the sense that my life was wasted, insignificant, meaningless.

To walk away now was to return to that life, but this book was something precious, valuable enough to be hidden, a secret that perhaps I could unlock.

I crawled around the altar, examining the flagstones for any evidence that they had been lifted. The dust and grime of years layered my frantic fingers as I searched, and finally, I found a place that had been brushed clean.

A strange symbol marked the stone, a curling filigree of loops ending in a forked demon's tail. It had cracked through the center, revealing a cleft at the side. My heart pounded with excitement as I levered it open.

As the violet light touched the stone with a sickly haze, I saw the book. A visceral desire to possess it rose within me, and I lifted it from its resting place, pulling it to my chest like a long-lost lover. The cover was soft leather, a patchwork of colors reminiscent of the varieties of human skin. It smelled of ancient herbs, a heady scent of rich tombs and incense disguising the darker note of death.

The pages opened beneath my eager hands and I tried to read the first words aloud. They were strange-sounding in my mouth, but within a few lines I could not hold back the torrent that flooded out. It was as if the book spoke through me and as my voice grew stronger, the sound echoed in the nave of the deserted place, rivaling even the power of the storm that raged outside.

As I reached the end of the powerful prayer, the world seemed to tremble and split. Sounds of lamentation filled the air. I crouched down, utterly terrified, screwing my eyes tight shut, trying to block the cacophony with my hands over my ears. Words of agony assaulted my mind, horrible dialects with the sounds of pounded flesh, as tortured spirits howled like dogs on the hunt, fangs bared to tear apart their prey.

Then all at once, it was over.

I heard soft footsteps in the silence that followed and looked up.

Emerging from a side chapel, where I had thought lay only tombs, came the young woman from the photograph who had danced with such abandon all those years ago with the handsome author.

Her long silken hair hung loose with flowers wound within as if she had just woken from dappled sleep on the banks of a sparkling stream. Her skin glowed with an internal light like alabaster from an Egyptian tomb, and her full lips were a deep peony pink. Her eyes were blue as a cornflower meadow, languid like a summer day. She exuded innocence with an edge of erotic knowing, and as she walked closer, I could scarcely draw breath. She pressed herself against me, her cool hand feathering down my chest to my belt.

"Through me, there is everything you desire in this life," she whispered, as her hand moved lower. "You only have to write it on your skin, and it will be yours." Her lips touched mine, her tongue darting out to lick delicately at the corner of my mouth. "There is only one tiny thing I want in return."

My lips opened against hers. I pushed all thought of Faerwald's bloated body from my mind, for surely his diary could only be the ravings of a madman.

CHAPTER 2:
SINS OF TREACHERY

30 years later.

THE PRIEST INTONED THE Canticle Benedictus, his breath freezing in the air as the solid oak casket was lowered into the hardened ground. Simon bent to pick up a handful of damp earth to throw on the coffin, holding the grainy soil in his palm. He focused on the ground, taking a moment to breathe through the wave of grief.

A thud of earth on wood.

Simon looked up quickly as someone else performed the family honor for the dead. When he saw who it was, the forgotten soil spilled from his hand.

Gest, his errant twin, had finally returned, but only after the death of the man who raised them.

"Grant this mercy, O Lord, we beseech Thee, to Thy servant departed, that he may not receive in punishment the requital of his deeds who in desire did keep Thy will ..."

As the priest said the final prayers, Gest smiled across the grave, his pale hazel eyes and high cheek-bones a perfect mirror of Simon's own, yet somehow an air of superiority and entitlement set him apart. His black pea-coat was perfectly tailored and Simon was suddenly aware of his own ill-fitting suit borrowed for the occasion. At a superficial level, they were identical twins, but Simon had always felt like a pale imitation, a watery reflection of his brother's bright color. Jealousy rekindled within him, a remnant of childhood rivalry. Try as he might, Simon had never been able to take the place of the favored twin with his grandfather, despite his labor in the pursuit of the Great Work.

"May his soul, and the souls of all the faithful departed, through the mercy of God, rest in peace. Amen."

The gathered crowd mumbled Amen from bowed heads and began to move away from the grave. Simon shook hands and nodded appropriately as people spoke kindly to him of his grandfather. But his eyes kept straying to Gest, who stood silently by the grave, his tightly wound energy repelling any who thought to approach him. Finally, when the last of the mourners left, Simon walked to his brother's side. They stood together looking into the pit, a reminder of where all must finally rest.

"Why now?" Simon asked, his voice clipped, almost breaking.

"He sent me a letter asking me to come a few weeks' back. Said he had something for me, something you were unwilling to take to its conclusion." Gest turned, his eyes as cold as the grave. "Where is it?"

He put his hand on Simon's arm, fingers gripping tight. Memories of youth flooded back and Simon remembered their games, how his bruises and broken bones were always blamed on clumsiness, how Gest was praised for caring so much for his brother – the weaker twin, the slower twin, the twin less blessed. That hand was still able to crush and dominate.

Simon flinched, as the years peeled away. "It's back at the house."

* * *

The mansion would have been opulent once, but its grandeur had faded through many years of neglect. Gest strode ahead into the dark entrance hall, quick steps taking him into dusty rooms the brothers had run through together as children, hiding amongst the towering bookcases, their palaces of imagination.

"It really hasn't changed much." He ran a finger along the grimy mantelpiece. "Seriously Si, how have you managed to live in this gloomy place for so long?"

Simon watched his brother's mercurial movements, his confident stride. He had always been the saturnine twin, the dark opposite to Gest's golden sun.

"I've been helping Grandfather. You know how much his research meant to him, and now to me."

Gest laughed, and Simon felt his years of intellectual pursuit dismissed in a heartbeat.

He had heard rumors of how Gest had spent the last twelve years, his string of beautiful women and exotic travels funded by the wealth they were both supposed to inherit, his expensive taste paid for by ever-dwindling funds. Simon knew that lust had also ruled his grandfather's early life, but the old man had wanted something different as he aged, searching for power and fulfilment beyond material things. Simon desired influence far beyond his brother's petty pleasures, but there had been days when he had longed to lose himself in an orgy of flesh.

Gest shrugged. "How you live your life is your own choice. But I want what he promised me, then I'll leave you alone in this melancholic place."

"His gift is in the lab. It's been extended since you were last here." Simon walked ahead through the dilapidated hallway to a metal door and pushed it open. "This way."

The neglected main house was in stark contrast to the gleaming laboratory, secretly constructed, where no one would have suspected that Simon and his grandfather continued to pursue the Great Work of the alchemists. Cutting edge science mingled with the occult, chemical formulas jostling for position with the symbols of medieval hermetics.

Gest walked through the lab, glancing from side to side with little interest. He idly picked up a round-bottomed flask and swirled the ruby liquid within.

"Careful with that." Simon snatched the flask away and placed it carefully back onto its stand.

Gest moved around the end of the bench. "That's his book, isn't it?"

Simon turned to see Gest fingering his grandfather's most precious tome, open to a page of intricately detailed symbols inscribed with spidery handwriting around the edge.

"It's mine now. He gave it to me." Simon thought back to the night when he had ripped the book from his Grandfather's embrace. The old man begged to hold it once more, his arms outstretched in need, covered with tattoos of words he had never explained. His eyes were shadowed with dread as he reached for it, filled with sinister memories the man couldn't help but relive, but would never speak of aloud. Simon had thrust the vodka bottle at him, his grandfather's addiction the only way to quiet the old man, while he delved ever deeper into the esoteric mysteries within.

Simon watched anxiously as Gest picked up the book, desperate to tear it from his brother's irreverent hands. Its cover was a patchwork of different colored leather, sewn with cords and pulled tight like scars on a checkered board of human skin. The spine and pages were edged with gold, a work of art even without the precious words inside.

Turning away as if he cared nothing for the book, Simon walked to a large print on the wall. Intricately woven symbols of the planets, astrological signs and their alchemical metals were etched in pitch black upon a white background. The iron of Mars, the god of war, and Mercury's quicksilver, ruling planet of the twins of Gemini. He touched one side of the print and it swung from the wall to reveal a safe.

"So that's where the old bastard hid his treasure." Gest dropped the book with a thump onto the bench.

Simon reached into the safe, took a heavy manila envelope out, and handed it to his brother. "Grandfather always said this was for you, and that I wasn't to open it."

It had clearly been opened.

Gest arched one perfectly groomed eyebrow and Simon shrugged. "I didn't seriously believe you would come back for it."

Gest pulled the papers out of the envelope and frowned as he studied the pages, a combination of handwritten diary entries scrawled with notes and modern GPS printouts. He looked up with a question in his eyes.

Simon smiled with perverse pleasure at his brother's ignorance. "It's a map, or a series of them. Grandfather told me about it after his first heart attack. He pleaded with me to follow the directions, to take the path he always wanted to. He spent most of his life trying to work out the symbols in the book, and towards the end, he said he had finally discovered the key. But he was on so much morphine by then, I dismissed his ranting. That must have been when he sent the letter to you."

Gest spread the pages out on a worktop, scanning them quickly. "These look authentic, Si, and I'm sure you're aware of the state of the bank accounts. We need this or we're both finished."

"Even if it takes everything we have left?" Simon looked around at his beloved lab, wondering if the risk was worth it even as a desire rose within him to discover what lay at the end of the map.

Gest grinned, his eyes sparkling with a lust for adventure. "Even if it takes every cent. We'll get it back a thousand-fold. Remember Grandfather's stories, the ones he told us as boys by the fire as the wind howled outside. Diamonds and precious stones and gems without name, just waiting for us to pull them from the ice. Now we have the map to show us the way."

Gest embraced his brother, spinning him around the lab. Simon reluctantly gave into his merriment, smiling for the first time since his grandfather's death, finally understanding why the map had been left to his headstrong, reckless twin.

*   *   *

Two months later, Simon shook his head as he thought back to that moment in the lab, the beginning of this trip to the frozen wastelands of the far north.

The map had indicated a little-known stratum of caves within the Arctic Circle, but their ship could carry them no further and now they had to take dog sleds for the final section of the journey inland.

The expedition had drained the last of the bank loans that Gest secured against the mansion and the lab, and Simon cursed his own weakness at letting his brother mortgage his life's work. His jaw ached from days of clenching it, each thunk of ice crunching on the side of the hull reminded him of the miles of frozen water between them and civilization.

There was no going back.

The specialist team finished the last checks of the equipment they needed to carry inland, and Simon stood on the ice watching as the handlers brought the sled dog teams out from the ship. The Siberian Huskies and Alaskan Malamutes leapt about yelping, shaking their shaggy fur, tongues hanging out as their hot breath frosted the air. They were reminiscent of wolves with sharp teeth and thick fur, animals suited to this cruel environment, ready to do battle with Nature.

"Cry havoc," Simon whispered, "and let slip the dogs of war."

He zipped up his fur-lined coat, his hand skimming the top pocket where his name was sewn in violet letters to help the crew tell the identical twins apart. As if he could be mistaken for his brother, Simon thought, as he watched Gest arguing with the expedition leader, making sure the man followed his instructions to the letter.

Since his brother's attention was elsewhere, Simon bent to check the position of the book within his pack. He had wrapped it in multiple protective and waterproof layers, but he still felt a need to reaffirm its safety.

As he placed his hand upon it, a curious warmth emanated from within, a pulse that seemed to quicken as the book moved closer to its home. Simon looked up to see gusts of wind on the ice, swirling into figures like mutated angels as they reached for the book with misshapen hands. He blinked and they dissolved into eddies of chill air. Simon tightened the straps on his pack, pulling it closer to his body as the team readied to move out.

*   *   *

Later that day, the expedition leader called a halt as he and Gest checked their coordinates on the old paper map against the modern GPS. Simon peered around, squinting at the sun through his goggles, taking in their surroundings with a dawning sense of recognition. The shallow valley with a silhouette of icy hills around them matched one of the drawings in the book, crimson lines etched in a shaky hand that his grandfather had never been able to interpret.

With rising excitement, Simon stepped off his sled. He snapped on cross-country skis and headed towards the edge of the valley, using poles to spur himself onward. The barking and howling of dogs followed him and he heard Gest shout in alarm, but he wanted to be the first to confirm whether this was indeed the place in the drawing. He rushed ahead around a curve in the valley floor.

Before him, a precipice fell into a vast pit beneath a strange formation of ice cliffs reminiscent of a demon's head. A dank and foul-smelling waterfall crashed into the depths, the dark water a sharp contrast to the clear crystal they had found elsewhere. Stones the color of iron encrusted with mold edged around the volcanic crevasse. Steam poured from the hole, filling the air with a hot stench like decaying flesh. Simon stood on the rim, part of him desperate to turn and run, and yet a dark sense called to the murky depths below as he gazed down into the tumbling waters.

Gest arrived on his skis, panting a little with the exertion of catching his brother, his face clouded with annoyance at being left behind.

"The map says that the caves are accessible from the waterfall," Gest said, as if he had found the location. "We're going down there. We're close, I can feel it."

The rest of the expedition team arrived and soon the crew were busy hammering in equipment and setting up abseiling gear.

Gest was impatient and, as soon as he could, he descended first with his head-lamp on, ignoring the expedition leader's request for initial safety checks. As he disappeared beneath the lip of the waterfall, Simon hurried his own preparation, quickly following Gest over the edge.

He glanced down, watching as his brother ducked under an overhang into a concealed cavern, unhooking his safety ropes in order to move more freely. Simon felt a pulse of excitement at finding the cave, a throbbing that seemed to vibrate through his pack from the book. Could this really be the place?

As he reached the cavern entrance, a low moan echoed from within, a deep sound of horror that was scarcely human, then retching and coughing.

Simon unhooked his harness and hurried down the rocky corridor into the cavern, blue light filtering down as the walls turned to ice away from the heat of the waterfall. As his head lamp flickered and reflected off the surface, Simon caught a glimpse of his own face as if in a mirror, startling him with the resemblance to his twin. He rounded a corner to find Gest bent double as he threw up the remains of his meager breakfast, the smell of vomit permeating the chill of the cave. Gest pointed and Simon turned slowly, his head lamp illuminating what his brother had seen.

A cylindrical block of ice bisected the cavern. There were bodies inside, split open, hacked apart, frozen limbs protruding in bulges. Simon walked around it, breathing deeply, swallowing down the bile that filled his throat.

One man was split from chin to groin, his entrails

dragged from his body, his heart cut from his chest, mutilated intestines frozen into a tableau of agony. Another figure lay face down, his head crushed, his back torn open by claws that rent his spine, exposing bones through ragged flesh flayed from his body. Who – or what – had done this?

Gest leaned against the wall, his face pale. He took a swig of water to rinse his mouth and then spat it out onto the floor of the cave, where it swiftly froze. "What do you think happened to them?"

Simon pointed at one of the dead, his head twisted around to face the back of his body, eyes frozen open. The man's clothes were the style and fabric of an earlier generation. "Whatever it was, it happened a long time ago."

Gest took a deep breath. "Do you think Grandfather knew of this?"

Simon heard judgment in his brother's voice, but he only felt a growing kinship with his grandfather's quest.

He swung off his pack and removed the book of multi-hued leather. It seemed to pulse in his hands as Simon flicked through the pages looking for the handwritten notes he had glimpsed once and now perhaps began to understand. He found them and smoothed the page open.

It showed a rough map of the north with the label Hyperborea inscribed in blood and twin lightning bolts scrawled at the bottom. A demon squatted in the middle of the land mass, a creature of primal myth, six wings beating against the cold north wind.

His grandfather had never been able to explain what it meant but now Simon felt a heat rise from the book, a throb of latent power. Light emanated from it and Simon's vision flashed. He saw the cave floor awash with blood, bodies hacked apart as a team of explorers died at the hands of a possessed madman who fled alone with the book, claiming its power.

Gest shone his torch away from the corpses towards the back of the cave, where light reflected in sparkling facets of brilliant color.

"Radio above," he said, no longer focused on the wretched forms of the dead, but on the potential riches beyond. "Tell them to wait while we investigate further. We mustn't let anyone else see this."

The visions of violence dissipated with Gest's interruption and Simon found himself obeying in a daze. He walked to the mouth of the cavern and radioed that all was fine and they would report again in another hour. As he walked back through the cave of the dead, Simon tucked the book into his inner clothing, close to his heart, relishing the strength that he drew from its growing potency, his heart beat synchronising with its strange pulse.

As he reached the inner chamber, Gest turned, his face illuminated by the flashlight, eyes aflame with desire for limitless wealth. "Look Si, these are diamonds. This is where I rebuild my fortune ... Where *we* rebuild our fortune, brother. Together."

Simon nodded, moving closer to examine the gems

embedded in the ice wall. Behind the shining stones, he could see a darker shadow in the shape of an altar.

He sensed that it was the true goal and his excitement soared as he realized that the Great Work could indeed be finished. He would return the book to its rightful place and claim the reward beyond temporal riches, leaving the jewels to the greed of his twin.

Simon reached for his pack and unhooked his pickaxe. He gripped the handle and hefted its weight, giving it a few swings to test the action.

"Careful with that," Gest said, his voice imperious.

At his brother's tone, Simon felt a sudden desire for great physical strength, a need to turn his body into hard, powerful muscle. He was sick of being considered the studious weakling, disgusted with himself for allowing his brother's dominance for so long.

He swung the axe heavily into the wall and a thud resounded through the chamber. Simon levered a chunk of the bejeweled ice to the floor where Gest broke it into smaller pieces with a hammer and chisel, picking out the shining gems. They soon removed their outer jackets, working up a sweat in the small cave with their labor. The pile of jewels grew larger and Gest started to fill his rucksack.

With one giant swing, Simon broke through into an alcove carved by ancient human hands. He worked faster to hack away the remaining ice and revealed an altar of black stone carved with mysterious symbols. There was an indentation in the middle, and Simon instinctively knew that the book should be laid there.

Gest stood up to look more closely. "What is it? Do you think it's worth anything?"

Simon's rage erupted at his brother's disregard for the sacred. He turned in anger. Gest shrank back at his brother's expression, stretching out his hands in mock surrender.

"OK, OK. Let's just pack up the gems and get out of here. The team can come down and dig out the rest, but these jewels, we keep for ourselves."

As Gest bent to fasten his pack, Simon reached into his jacket for the book. He unwrapped the precious tome, dark pleasure rising within him as he touched its outer skin. With reverence, he placed it on the altar within the boundaries of the indentation. It fit perfectly and Simon knelt before it, bending his head in veneration.

Behind him, Gest snorted in derision at his actions.

As Simon rose and turned in anger, the chamber trembled, as if giants shook their limbs to free themselves from the ice.

A hail of rock fell from the ceiling and the brothers covered their heads. A chunk knocked Simon over and he landed heavily on his side, his skull smacking against the ground. His vision darkened and then cleared again as he sat up and rubbed his head, pain lancing through him.

The altar had split down the center of the rock beneath the book and icy vapor oozed out of the newly-formed crack, dissipating into the air. Afraid that the book would be damaged, Simon reached for it, breathing in the tainted air as he did so. It smelled metallic and he tasted blood in his mouth, then his senses sharpened and he heard a terrible howl pouring from the abyss below beneath the beating of demonic wings.

"We'd better hurry," Gest said, as if he couldn't hear the frenzied clamor or see the cloudy haze. "Clearly this cave isn't stable. We need to get the jewels out while we still can."

He forced another chunk of gemstone into his pack. It shone in the lamplight and Simon caught a glimpse of his brother's reflection.

Gest's handsome face turned into that of a hideous lizard and behind him, a curved scorpion's tail emerged from his ripped snowsuit. Simon fell back against the wall, watching as his twin's face morphed from the Gest he knew into a sinister visage of reptilian scales, forked tongue flickering in the air.

Something within him understood that this unholy demon was his brother's true nature revealed by the book. There was only one way he could stop it.

Simon surged forward, his strength amplified from within. He pushed his brother to the ground, raising the pick axe once more.

As Gest screamed in terror, Simon brought the weapon down. He became the avenger, the destroyer, hacking relentlessly at his brother's body as words from the precious book of skin ran through his mind.

Simon's breath was ragged as he finally cleaved the head from the mutilated torso, the ice slippery with gore as what remained of Gest's body began to harden with ice crystals.

Another tremor rocked the cavern. There was little time before it collapsed, concealing both riches and the murder within.

The two padded outer jackets lay side by side away from the bloody mess. Simon stood looking at them, thinking of the divergent lives that he and Gest had experienced. In that moment he saw a possible future, where earthly pleasure and power could be his as well as the Great Work fulfilled.

He removed his bloody top, chest exposed to the chill air, revealing a tattoo of an orb cupped within a bowl on top of an inverted cross. Simon tugged a fresh merino sweater from his pack, pulled it over his head and zipped Gest's jacket on over the top. He straightened his back, adopting his brother's proud posture, then he picked up the two heavy packs and headed for the waterfall. It was time to tell the crew that his brother Simon had perished within the cavern as it collapsed, despite his own desperate attempts at rescue.

Behind him, icy vapor rose from the altar, winding its way out of the ancient cavern into the world above.

CHAPTER 3:
SINS OF VIOLENCE

30 years later.

AN EXPLOSION ROCKED THE air, raining chunks of masonry and glass down from the building above. Ari and Sibyl dived behind the hulk of a ruined truck, rolling underneath to shelter from the hail of debris.

"It's getting closer." Sibyl's voice was tinged with the longing for battle, and Ari knew her friend wanted to be back there, fighting deep in Sector 35. The Corps was the only family they had now, a renegade team trying to restore order to a tiny corner of the desolate planet.

Once the dust had settled, Ari rolled out from under the vehicle. "The war won't end while we take a few hours off." She sprang to her feet, her lithe body as fast as a wild cat.

"Time off?" Sibyl laughed as she brushed herself down. "I haven't heard that expression since before the Contagion."

"Come on. We need to keep moving." Ari scanned the scene, acutely aware that they were off their patch, deep into Untamed territory, but she had to risk running this gauntlet. It was almost too late.

The message had arrived a few days before, passed through the networks that kept communication alive on this forsaken continent. Elyse was about to be Blessed, and Ari couldn't let that happen. Even though she hadn't seen her sister for fifteen years, she still remembered her blonde curls and the way her skin smelled after a bath, back in the days when they were still possible. The little girl's innocent giggle stuck most in her mind, the last thing she heard before she was led away for her own Blessing.

She would not let that same violation happen to Elyse.

Ari and Sibyl darted between the ruined buildings of the Empty Quarter, eyes drawn to every shadow. The area was only designated empty so that it could be written out of any rescue plan, but Ferals lurked here among the Untamed and plague victims eked out a pitiful existence in its shattered world.

"You've never told me what happened back then," Sibyl said.

Ari looked ahead, avoiding her gaze. "I'll tell you when I come back out again." *If I come back out again.* "It's a long story. Thanks for coming with me."

Sibyl shook her head, dismissing the gratitude. "Just don't expect me to stop asking for some answers."

They walked on, alert for danger. The Empty Quarter had once been a business hub, with high-rise office buildings, boutique shops and restaurants. A center of commerce in the days when people had First World concerns – could they afford private education for their children? Which new car would be most fuel efficient and safe?

Those were the days when people didn't need to know practical skills like how to grow crops or fix farm equipment, or even how to fight and defend their families. The end of that life had come before Ari was born, but she had seen its reflection in her mother's eyes as she stumbled to draw water daily from the public well. Her mother's naivety in the face of disaster had resulted in her own birth, a child of rape in the days when defense of the country became more important than protecting the innocent within its borders.

Now the Turning was legend, with many tales told of how the days of plenty had been ended by the Contagion.

The mysterious illness had spread from the icy far north, at first considered a wave of extreme violence endemic only to isolated communities. But when ordinary families were slaughtered by soccer Moms and children hacked their school friends to death, the authorities began to study the nascent brutality. They found a virus, a strain unseen before, that turned the infected into savage, uninhibited killers.

They scrambled for containment, but the virus was

airborne and soon reached the larger urban populations of the Northern Hemisphere. It spread quickly, taking millions in its bloody wake. International disputes erupted in the panic, blame heaped upon whichever nation was considered a sworn enemy. Humanity had only ever been a splinter away from chaos.

It wasn't long before the combat went nuclear, wiping out major cities where most of the infrastructure and knowledge resided. The world was split apart, and now humanity dwelled in the ashes.

Ari and Sibyl walked quickly along the edge of the road, where the buckling and cracking were less pronounced, and they could use the crenelated buildings as cover.

Sibyl pointed to a graffitied wall at a symbol painted in pitch, its edges dripping like black blood. An orb cupped in a bowl on top of an inverted cross, representing the God of the Underworld who had stolen the hope of summer from the earth.

"Is that his Mark?"

Ari looked up and memories flooded back from the night of her Blessing when that symbol had been seared into her brain. The Fallen Ones had held her down as she writhed, while the sound of a thousand fiendish angels cursed and screamed for her corruption.

Ari nodded. "He calls this place the city of Dis, supposedly guarded by fallen angels, punished by God for their disobedience. The Mark encircles his domain."

The Contagion had separated the remnant of

humanity into those who turned away from the idea of deity, and those who believed it was God's judgment for the sins of the world. But Ari knew the truth. There was no God here, only one man's brutality, and the shadows were ever deepening.

She looked up at the sky. "We must hurry. The Blessing begins as the sun dips below the horizon."

They started a slow jog towards the walls that loomed in the distance, where fires burned on the ramparts proclaiming the city's dominion over the scarred land. Their feet beat in time, their even breath creating a rhythm born from years together in the Corps.

The city of Dis had grown like a cancer inside the walls of an old power station that had once been luxurious flats in the days Before. In the chaos of the last generation, factions sprang up, and people aligned themselves with warlords who fought for dominance. The man who ruled Dis had a name back then, but now he was known only as The Minotaur. He lived at the centre of the labyrinth that the city had become, and he called the prettiest girls to its heart for the Blessing.

As they jogged on, Ari glanced up at the trees growing alongside this stretch of road, emerging roots thrusting through concrete. Nature thrived as humanity was all but destroyed. Trees like these were their refuge most nights, their home on many a mission for the Corps. Ari craved the security of those branches now, but she forced herself on.

A patch of thorny bushes loomed ahead. They were

too far away to see clearly, but they seemed to be hung with scraps of material.

As they drew closer, Ari's heart crumpled as she realized what they were. Corpses hung on the barbs, hooking into skin that had been cut and maimed, in various stages of decomposition. They hung along the main road to the city, traitors or blasphemers against the perverted laws of the Minotaur.

Ari reached for Sibyl's hand as they stood before the ruined bodies, and tears gathered in her eyes. Those of the Goddess considered life to be more precious after the Contagion but within the boundaries of Dis, life was expendable. As they walked past the dead hand in hand, Ari felt a deep sense of guilt at leaving these people behind to their brutal fate.

"You were only a child when you escaped," Sibyl said softly. "If you hadn't left, you would have ended up bearing that monster's children, or dead out here with words of defiance carved into your flesh."

As Ari nodded slowly, she noticed a glimmer of color in the shadows. At the base of one of the bushes, a single rose bloomed, its petals stained red with the blood of the martyrs. Ari bent to stroke its leaves and breathe in the faint scent, a sign from the Goddess, hope of new life in this dark valley of the dead.

They walked on within the shadow of the protective trees and ducked into one of the ruined buildings before they came within sight of the guard towers of Dis. Ari took off her pack and pulled out a dress she had found only days before, slightly stained with blood but cut well enough to make the guards open the door for a closer look.

She stripped off her camouflage uniform and pulled on the dress.

"That's hideous." Sibyl stuffed her rough hands deep into her pockets, fists clenched.

Ari untied her hair from its scarf, letting her dark curls hang loose. "The only guaranteed way into Dis is as breeding stock. I know how it works in there. I need the guards to take me to him immediately."

She pulled her dog-tags from around her neck and held them out, the symbol of the Corps glinting in the afternoon light.

Sibyl shook her head. "I have enough of those from sisters lost." She sighed, then took the dog-tags with reluctance. "Please don't go."

Ari pulled Sibyl into an embrace. and they stood, hearts beating together. There was so much to say, but no time left, not now. After a few moments, they broke apart. Ari knew she must act now or she would give in to her fear, turn and run and leave this place behind forever.

"I'm coming back, and I'm bringing Elyse with me, so I need you outside to cover our retreat and help us get away. Inside there, you'd be a liability. You don't know it like I do. I'm sorry, but I have to go alone." Ari took Sibyl's hands once more, her eyes serious. "Promise me you'll move to a tree near the gate after dark, and stay there? If I'm not out by first light, I'm not coming out at all. Leave and get back to the Corps. Promise me."

"Alright, alright." Sibyl brushed away tears. "Enough now. Get in and get out again. I'll be waiting."

Ari limped out of the building, feigning weakness as she neared the forbidding doors of Dis. They were fortified from the ruins of conquered enclaves, and now the ornate, triumphal arch had become a portal to the Minotaur's Hell, where the violent prospered, and the weak could only do his bidding.

Ari recalled the expression of fear on the murdered bodies and painted her own face with the same as she approached. Her heart pounded, her ears filled with the sound of her own blood as two guardsmen came out to meet her, eyes hard as they raked over her body. One held a ferocious dog on a short leash, its powerful jaws slavering, ready to charge and tear flesh on command.

Ari pleaded for sanctuary. She was just a woman trying to stay alive and this was her last chance for refuge. She knew it was how so many arrived here and did not emerge to the sun again.

One of the guards nodded, and Ari walked quickly through the gate before he changed his mind. The great doors slammed shut behind her, the sound of a prison cell closing. Panic rose within as her vision narrowed. She was trapped here away from the sight of the sky, out of reach of the Goddess, but it was too late to go back now.

"Take her up to him quickly," one of the guards said

to two others. "He'll be with the young one tonight, so he'll likely send her back down to us quick smart." His leer transformed his face into the mugshot of a demon, the corruption of the city made flesh. "But don't worry, princess, we'll take good care of you. Won't we, boys?"

With raucous laughter echoing behind her, two guards pulled Ari deeper into the stronghold of Dis, her footsteps treading ground she had sworn never to walk on again. She glanced up at the walkways stretching into four great towers above. They were crowded with people walking slowly about their labor, too exhausted to even look down at her, too burned out to be curious. Entropy ruled here, decay and decline evident in the stink of the overcrowded population, kept wretched by the fear of what was outside the walls in the dark.

The Minotaur used narcotics to keep the population subdued, over-riding human will with a desperation to merely survive each day. The cheapest of the drugs, known as Vir-Gil, was cut with chemicals that burned skin and corrupted blood. Deformity seeped into the population birth by birth, so refugee women with fresh blood were always in demand.

Ari could see the imprint of what the city had once been, but the place had changed in her long absence. The colors were now a palate of grey and brown, not the burnt sienna of autumn leaves or the silver feathers of the mountain owl, but bleached and faded versions of the natural world of the Goddess. The world outside was difficult and dangerous indeed, but wasn't it better to die in the woods as the sun filtered down through the leaves, a last moment of pleasure before the end? There was nothing left of beauty here, except perhaps the children, before they were ruined even as they bloomed. Enough. Ari fixed her gaze on the back of the guard's head, counting the minutes until she stood before the monster once again.

At the heart of the city, fragile huts packed with families formed a labyrinth, the jagged paths through the shanty town near impossible to navigate. It stank of sewage and decay. People fled at the guards' approach, shrinking against flimsy shelters, darting into shadows to avoid the batons that could come down at any point. The cowering figures were branded with his Mark, the burns of ownership black and ragged on their skin.

Ari followed the guards past pits like open tombs, where heretics against the Minotaur were thrown to fight and die, as flaming coals were flung upon them. Men shouted around the edges, betting what little they had on the brawling below, witnesses to a battle that could only end in death.

At the edge of the shanty town, the guards led Ari up rungs of steel inside one of the main towers, their lewd comments soon silenced by physical exertion. As she climbed, part of her wanted to smash her boot down into the face of the guard below, kick him off into the gaping space so that his body dashed on the ground beneath, giving the pitiful crowd some hope of defiance. She squashed those feelings down. Her ill-timed bravado would not help Elyse.

She forced her arms to pull faster, finally arriving on a wide platform that looked out over the city below, with a window to the ruined world outside and a single door.

One of the guards knocked, the sound echoing down the deep shaft below. Ari glanced out of the window to the horizon, the rim of the sun only inches away from dipping lower. Another few minutes and the ritual would begin. Her heart beat faster at the sound of approaching footsteps.

The door opened to reveal a young girl, eyes downcast, body hunched. Was this Elyse? Ari scanned her features. No, she would be in preparation, so this must be the one she would replace. As the Minotaur of ancient Greece, the monster of Dis took new life each month to serve his needs, before discarding the old to the pandemonium below.

"He's busy," the girl whispered. "You cannot disturb him now."

Ari stepped forward. "He'll want to see me. Tell him a lost daughter has returned to beg for his mercy."

The girl's eyes flickered upwards, meeting Ari's gaze with a glimmer of recognition. Perhaps they had heard tales of her escape. Perhaps she had unwittingly provided a hope of freedom beyond the gates.

The guard turned, his hand raised to strike her for impudence. Ari stood tall to face him, waiting for the blow.

"Enough." A deep voice came from within, and Ari shivered in recognition. "She may enter."

The guard paled and dropped his arm, pushing Ari to the door, keeping his eyes lowered.

Ari walked in, and there he was, the man she had feared all her life, who had roamed her nightmares since the day she had run from this place, wounded from his Blessing.

He stepped from the shadows, his broad chest bare and oiled emphasizing the tattooed Mark, the symbol of his domination. He was still magnificent, his height and strength giving him an advantage over any man who would challenge him in the pit.

But there were more scars on his body now and touches of grey in his thick hair. Ari realized that he was just a man, not the eternal monster of her childish dreams.

"Ariadne." His voice was a filthy caress. "I thought you dead many years ago." He stepped forward, his dark eyes compelling. "Kneel."

Ari found herself obeying without resistance and she fell to her knees as he approached. His fingers lifted her chin, caressed her lips, then twisted into her hair, pulling it tight.

"Who is the traitor that tells of your sister's Blessing?" The Minotaur tugged her head back, pulling a knife from his belt, holding it against the flesh of her neck.

Ari's heart raced. Her pulse beat against the blade as she sent a desperate prayer to the Goddess.

He stroked the knife gently over Ari's delicate skin, raising a bead of blood that trickled down into the top of her dress. His eyes watched as it ran over the swell of her breast, then he let go, pushing her roughly forwards. "No matter, I will find out after the ritual is complete. Tonight you will witness your sister's Blessing."

He snapped his fingers. Three women emerged from the shadows, their bodies tattooed with serpents, their hair twisted into tight rings on top of their heads.

"Meet my Furies." He walked away, laughing over his shoulder. "Did you really think I would remain in my eyrie without protection? They were chosen from the death pits, the ones who remained standing after the Purge." He turned to the women. "Bring her."

As the Minotaur strode away up a staircase to the rooftop, Ari backed away from the Furies, crouching into a defensive posture. The women undulated closer, their bodies sinuous. They had the crazed dilated pupils of junkies, addicted to the drugs and violence that kept this city of ruined souls alive.

"I want to follow him," Ari said, still backing away, fighting to keep her voice even. Her eyes darted to each Fury, judging their distance. "You don't need to drag me up there."

"Now, where's the fun in that?" one of the Furies said, her lips drawn back in a vicious grin as the three of them edged forwards.

Ari tried to block their attack, but they were too

many. A blow to the kidney opened her up for a punch to the stomach. She fell to her knees, winded and gasping for air. One Fury held her head up by the hair, and another readied her fist to strike.

"Not her face," the other said, her voice tinged with fear. "He won't like that."

The Fury satisfied herself with another gut punch, and Ari crumpled to the ground in agony. The women dragged her up the staircase, emerging onto a platform that perched atop the tower with views of the ruined land beyond.

A cool breeze blew across the deck, and the Furies raised their faces to the sky, drinking in the fresh air that was denied them in the depths of the stinking city. They held Ari tight, fingernails digging into her flesh, two of them with knives drawn. The sun burned the horizon, just a touch above sinking below it. As the last rays reached them, Ari saw her sister.

Elyse was tied to the altar on the edge of the platform, with nothing but air between her and the Goddess. Her limbs were lashed down, and she struggled weakly, her blonde hair spread out on the carved wooden shrine to his foul god. At the four corners of the altar stood dark angel figures, but now Ari could see that they were only metal sculptures, not real men. Those jagged wings had haunted her nightmares, but now she saw through the artifice, manufactured by hallucinogens the girls were forced to take, their minds corrupted while he took his malevolent pleasure.

The Minotaur stood on the edge of the tower, looking out towards the burning plains as the dying sun lit the earth with a ruby glow and a touch of flame. It seemed as if flakes of fire rained down upon a river of blood that weaved across the ruined landscape below, a breath-taking moment of beauty from the Goddess. He read aloud from a book of human skin, its patchwork of color catching the light, transforming its curses into a parody of sunburst.

As the Minotaur spoke the final words, he lifted the great helmet upon his head, with horns that Ari still saw in her fevered nightmares. The Furies gazed towards him, mesmerized, as his body was lit by the dying sun, his bronzed, muscled skin alive with fire.

In that moment, Ari knew what she must do.

She spun from the grasp of one Fury, pushing her away into another. As they stumbled back, Ari felt the bite of a blade on her arm as one of them slashed down, but she was out of their grip. Time slowed as she saw the Minotaur's eyes widen at the sound of struggle, and she glimpsed human frailty there. He was but a man, lord of this nest of malice, but still only a man.

Ari ran at him, her legs swift from the fitness of the Corps, the years she had spent training for just this moment. At the last second, she jumped, using the corner of the altar to give her leverage against his bulk. As his arms wrapped around her body, his roar of anger exploded, and together they toppled over the edge into the void.

As they fell, Ari looked out towards the dying sun, into the very face of the Goddess, his screams of rage her final prayer.

THE END

AUTHOR'S NOTE

THESE SHORT STORIES WERE originally written as part of an online competition, *The Descent*, run by Kobo, an online ebook and audiobook retailer, for the launch of Dan Brown's thriller, *Inferno*.

The Descent was based on Dante's *Inferno* and these stories featured as the opening to a transmedia game that linked to special websites, using symbols, words and numbers from the story as clues to the next step.

My brief was to write three interlinking stories using the symbolism of Dante's *Inferno*, grouped into the main categories of sin. I love research so this was a fun project!

In this collection, the stories have been re-ordered to represent the passage of time, with the book of human skin linking the generations who possess it. There are layers of symbolism in the stories as described below, and you can see related images at:

www.pinterest.com/jfpenn/dante-inferno

I re-edited the stories for audiobook production in 2019.

Language and imagery used by Dante in Inferno

As part of my research, I read a modern translation of Dante's *Inferno* and made notes on the text, writing down images and specific words to use in my stories that would echo the rings of Hell.

In *Sins of the Flesh*, the bloated dead body of the tattooed author echoes the Gluttonous who lie in a "vile slush of ceaseless foul." The images of the Lustful on the wall and the stormy valley crossing reflect the souls blown back and forth by wind with no rest.

The desecrated church is my own, inspired by reading H.P. Lovecraft horror stories.

In *Sins of Treachery*, Simon whispers "Cry havoc, and let slip the dogs of war," spoken by Anthony after the murder of Julius Caesar in Shakespeare's play of the same name. The traitors who led that insurrection are in the deepest circle of Inferno, in the mouth of Satan himself.

The Arctic location echoes Dante's Hell which is encased in ice, and the entrance is through a 'precipice of dark-tinted water'. The tortured, distorted bodies of the men in the ice pillar reflect the terrible wounds of the treacherous and the fraudulent, some torn apart and disemboweled by demons for eternity.

In *Sins of Violence*, the city of Dis itself is portrayed, surrounding the lower parts of Hell in Dante's original.

The bodies on the thorn bushes are suicides in *Inferno*, but I use them here as a device to show the depravity of the ruler. The Minotaur and the Furies also come from the original, as do the heretics in their burning graves within the city, albeit used in a different form.

The title of the collection comes from Canto VIII, where 'a thousand fiendish angels' sit perched on the gates of the city.

Symbolism

Occult and mythological symbols were used to evoke the atmosphere of *Inferno* and also to lead to further clues within the original *Descent* game.

In *Sins of the Flesh*, the door covered in occult symbols includes the medal of St Benedict, a Catholic sacramental medal used to ward off evil.

The images on the walls are from Khajuraho, a real Hindu temple in Madhya Pradesh, India, which is carved with images of explicit sexual positions. William Blake's Circle of the Lustful is a watercolor depicting a whirling vortex of naked lovers.

The symbol on the flagstone that hides the book is the Seal of Asmodeus, King of Demons from the Book of Tobit and also mentioned in the Talmud.

In *Sins of Treachery*, symbols of the planets, astrological signs and their alchemical metals are shown on the safe door, featuring the iron of Mars, the god of war, and Mercury's quicksilver, ruling planet of the twins of Gemini.

In *Sins of Violence*, the Mark of the Minotaur is an orb cupped in a bowl on top of an inverted cross, the symbol for Pluto, God of the Underworld.

Names of characters

In *Sins of the Flesh*, the dead author is Christopher Faerwald. Dante's *Inferno* is the story of a traveler through the circles of Hell. Christopher is the patron saint of travelers, while Faerwald is an old English word for traveler.

In *Sins of Treachery*, Simon Magus is punished in the Eighth circle of Hell for Fraud, and Gestas was the impenitent thief crucified alongside Jesus, greedy for more.

In *Sins of Violence*, Ariadne helped Theseus kill the Minotaur, although I portray her as the heroine in my story. The name of the drug Vir-Gil is homage to Dante's guide through *Inferno*, the poet Virgil.

ENJOYED THE STORIES?

Thanks for reading *A Thousand Fiendish Angels*. I hope you enjoyed the stories and a review on the store where you bought the book would be much appreciated.

If you'd like to try more of my books, you can get a free copy of my bestselling supernatural thriller, *Day of the Vikings*, when you sign up to join my Reader's Group.

You'll also be notified of giveaways, new releases, and receive personal updates from behind the scenes of my books.

WWW.JFPENN.COM/FREE

* * *

Day of the Vikings, an ARKANE thriller

*A ritual murder on a remote island under the
shifting skies of the aurora borealis.*

A staff of power that can summon Ragnarok, the Viking apocalypse.

When Neo-Viking terrorists invade the British Museum in London to reclaim the staff of Skara Brae, ARKANE agent Dr. Morgan Sierra is trapped in the building along with hostages under mortal threat.

As the slaughter begins, Morgan works alongside psychic Blake Daniel to discern the past of the staff, dating back to islands invaded by the Vikings generations ago.

Can Morgan and Blake uncover the truth before Ragnarok is unleashed, consuming all in its wake?

Day of the Vikings is a fast-paced, supernatural thriller set in London and the islands of Orkney, Lindisfarne and Iona. Set in the present day, it resonates with the history and myth of the Vikings.

If you love an action-packed thriller,
you can get Day of the Vikings for free now:

WWW.JFPENN.COM/FREE

Day of the Vikings features Dr. Morgan Sierra from the ARKANE thrillers, and Blake Daniel from the London Crime Thrillers, but it is also a stand-alone novella that can be read and enjoyed separately.

MORE BOOKS BY J.F.PENN

If you like **action adventure thrillers with a supernatural edge**, check out the **ARKANE** series as Morgan Sierra and Jake Timber solve supernatural mysteries around the world.

Stone of Fire #1
Crypt of Bone #2
Ark of Blood #3
One Day In Budapest #4
Day of the Vikings #5
Gates of Hell #6
One Day in New York #7
Destroyer of Worlds #8
End of Days #9
Valley of Dry Bones #10

Available in ebook, print, and audiobook editions as well as boxsets.

* * *

If you like **crime thrillers with an edge of the supernatural**, join Detective Jamie Brooke and museum researcher Blake Daniel, in the London crime thriller trilogy:

Desecration #1
Delirium #2
Deviance #3

Available in ebook, print, and audiobook editions as well as boxsets.

* * *

If you enjoy **dark fantasy,** check out:

Map of Shadows, a Mapwalker novel #1
Risen Gods
American Demon Hunters: Sacrifice

A Thousand Fiendish Angels: Short stories based on Dante's Inferno

The Dark Queen: An archaeological short story

More books coming soon.

If you loved the book and have a moment to spare,
I would really appreciate a short review on the page
where you bought the book. Your help in spreading
the word is gratefully appreciated and reviews make a
huge difference to helping new readers find the series.

Thank you!

ABOUT J.F.PENN

J.F.Penn is the Award-nominated, New York Times and USA Today bestselling author of the ARKANE supernatural thrillers, London Crime Thrillers, and the Mapwalker dark fantasy series, as well as other stand-alone stories.

Her books weave together ancient artifacts, relics of power, international locations and adventure with an edge of the supernatural. Joanna lives in Bath, England and enjoys a nice G&T.

*   *   *

You can sign up for a free thriller,
Day of the Vikings, and updates from behind the
scenes, research, and giveaways at:

WWW.JFPENN.COM/FREE

* * *

Connect at:
www.JFPenn.com
joanna@JFPenn.com
www.Facebook.com/JFPennAuthor
www.Instagram.com/JFPennAuthor
www.Twitter.com/JFPennWriter

* * *

For writers:

Joanna's site, www.TheCreativePenn.com, helps people write, publish and market their books through articles, audio, video and online courses.

She writes non-fiction for authors under Joanna Penn and has an award-nominated podcast for writers, The Creative Penn Podcast.

ACKNOWLEDGMENTS

A huge thank you to Mark Leslie Lefebvre from Kobo for thinking of me when this opportunity arose and for being an enthusiastic advocate for authors, as well as a fantastic horror writer himself.

Also thanks to Kobo's marketing team, who created such a brilliant competition and for making the stories even more resonant with symbolism through the editing process. I really enjoyed working with you all.

Thanks to my cover designer, Jane Dixon Smith from JDSmithDesign, and to Liz Broomfield at LibroEditing for proof-reading.

Thanks to Peter Warnock for the voice training sessions that helped me narrate the audiobook version, and to Dan Van Werkhoven for mastering the audio files.

The biggest thank you goes out to my readers. I hope to keep pushing the edge of what I write.